BORIS
the brainiest baby

ORCHARD BOOKS
96 Leonard Street, London EC2A 4RH
Orchard Books Australia
14 Mars Road, Lane Cove, NSW 2066

First published in Great Britain in 1997
First paperback publication 1998

A CIP catalogue record for this book is available from the
British Library.
1 86039 553 8 (hardback)
1 86039 625 9 (paperback)
Printed in Great Britain

BORIS
the brainiest baby

Laurence Anholt

Illustrated by Tony Ross

ORCHARD BOOKS

We are going to meet Boris.
We are going to meet Boris, the brainiest baby ever born. I cannot tell you how brainy Boris is. He is just too brainy for words.

The minute Boris was born, he shook hands with the doctor and kissed his mother. "Good morning," he said. "I am Boris, the brainiest baby ever born."

All the nurses in the hospital came running. They had never seen a new baby dress himself.

Boris put on a tiny suit.

Boris put on a tiny bow-tie.

Boris took a tiny umbrella and
Boris stepped outside.

"Boris, you are too young to leave the hospital," said his mother and father and all the doctors. "You are only one hour old."

"Nonsense!" said Boris. "I am Boris, the brainiest baby ever born. I have many things to do. Please call a taxi."

When they arrived home, his mother tried to give Boris a big cuddle and a sloppy kiss.

But Boris didn't have time for cuddles or sloppy kisses. He had to get to school.

“Boris you are too young to go to school,” said his father. “You are only one morning old.”

“Nonsense!” said Boris. “I am Boris, the brainiest baby ever born. Here comes the school bus. Goodbye.”

Boris liked it at school. The teacher showed him a nice picture-book. "Look, Boris. Here is a woof-woof and a quack-quack," she said.

“Nonsense!” said Boris. “That is not a woof-woof. And that is not a quack-quack. It is a dog and a duck. It is time you learnt the proper words.”

"This baby is too brainy," said the teacher. "This baby is too brainy to be at school."

So Boris went home. His father came to tuck him into his cot. But Boris was on the telephone. "I'm finished with school," said Boris. "Now I'm trying to find a job."

“Boris, you are too young to get a job,” said his mother and father. “You are only one day old.”

"Nonsense!" said Boris. "I am Boris, the brainiest baby ever born. My train leaves in the morning. Goodnight."

The next day, Boris took a train to the city.
He started work at a big office at the top of a high tower.

"Good morning, everybody," said Boris. "I am Boris, the brainiest baby ever born. Let's make money."

Boris liked it at the office. He had a big desk and lots of telephones.

At lunchtime, his mother came to change his nappy and give him a hug. Boris was far too busy on the computer.

"Perhaps there will be time for a hug at the weekend," said Boris. "Please talk to my secretary."

The people at the office said,
"This baby is too brainy to work
in our office. He should be the
boss of our company."

That evening, Boris came home late. His mother and father were waiting up. They had bought him

a pink fluffy bunny.

"I am too busy for bunnies," said Boris. "I am the boss of a big company. I have to fly away for an important meeting. The aeroplane leaves in one hour. I must pack my bag."

"Boris, you are too young to be the boss of a big company," said his mother and father. "You are only two days old."

"Nonsense!" said Boris.
That night he flew in an aeroplane to another country. Boris liked going to other countries. Boris liked learning to speak new languages.

The Prime Minister of the country came to see Boris, the brainiest baby ever born.

"You are too brainy to be the boss of a big company," said the Prime Minister. "You should be a Prime Minister like me."

"Yes!" shouted all the people. "You should be a Prime Minister like him."

So Boris flew back. He began to feel very tired. He wished he had his pink bunny.

At home, his mother and father had painted some fluffy lambs on his nursery wall.

"I expect you are ready for a nap and a cuddle now," said Boris's father.

Boris thought for a moment. He thought it would be nice to have a nap and a cuddle in the nursery with the fluffy lambs on the wall.

But Boris said, “No. I am Boris, the brainiest baby ever born. I am going to be Prime Minister. I am going to go on television to talk to everyone. The show starts in ten minutes.”

Lots of people came to the house. There were bright lights and television cameras and lots of noise.

Everybody was ready to start. Everybody in the country was sitting at home watching TV.

They wanted to see Boris. They wanted to see Boris, the brainiest baby ever born. They wanted to see Boris, the Prime Minister.

But Boris had gone. Nobody could find him.

The people looked everywhere. They ran all over the house with their television cameras.

Boris was not on the telephone.

Boris was not on his computer.

Boris was not ready to talk on the television.

At last they found him. Boris was in the nursery with the fluffy lambs on the wall.

"Sssh!" said his mother.
"Sssh!" said his father.

Boris was cuddled up in his mother's arms with his pink bunny.

Boris, the brainiest baby ever born, was fast asleep.
After all, he was only four days old.